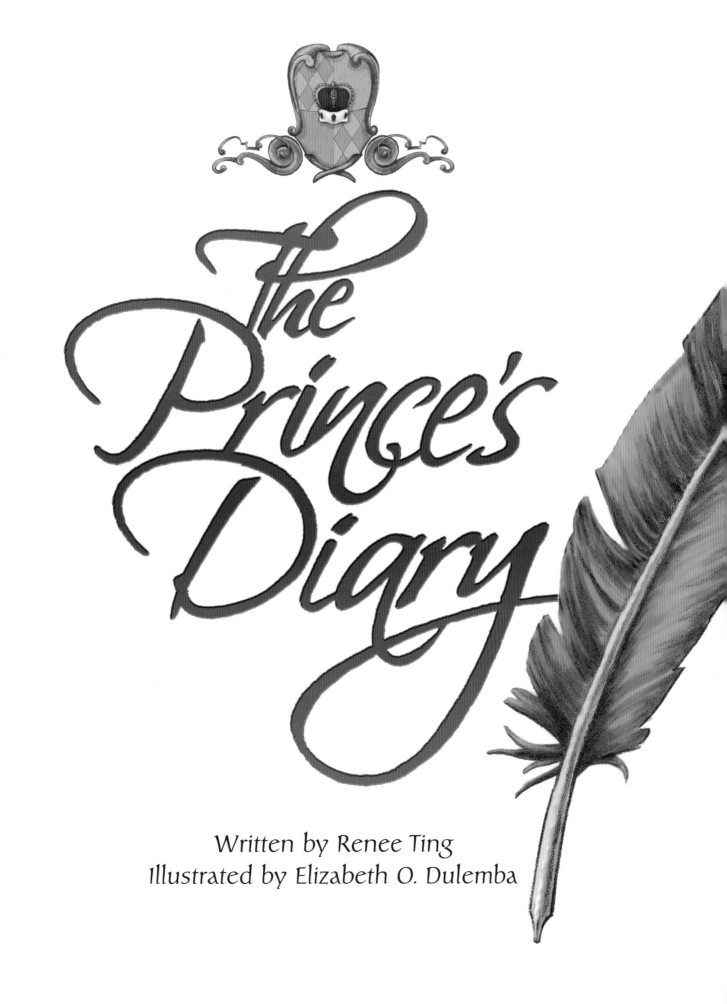

The Prince's Diary

Written by Renee Ting
Illustrated by Elizabeth O. Dulemba

Library of Congress Cataloging-in-Publication Data

Ting, Renee.
The Prince's Diary / Renee Ting ; illustrated by Elizabeth O. Dulemba.
   p. cm.
 Summary: In this version of the Cinderella tale, the Prince tells his
side of the story through diary entries.
 ISBN 1-885008-27-9
 [1. Princes--Fiction. 2. Diaries--Fiction.] I. Dulemba, Elizabeth O.,
ill. II. Title.
 PZ7.T4887Pr 2005
 [E]--dc22

                        2004024861

Shen's Books
Fremont, California

Printed in China

Text design and computer production: Patty Arnold, Menagerie Design and Publishing

For my parents, who are always there for me. —R.T.
For Stan, my Prince Charming. —E.D.

June 4

I have fallen in love with the most beautiful girl, but I don't even know her name!

I was riding Silver by the creek this morning when I saw a girl fetching water. I hid behind a tree so I could watch her without her seeing me. Her clothes were old and worn, and there was a smudge of dirt on her cheek, but still she was beautiful. She even lugged bucketfuls of water gracefully.

I think I'll call her Cinderella.

June 10

I spent the entire morning helping Father with the kingdom accounting. What a bore! At least our kingdom is a small one, so there isn't that much paperwork to do.

As soon as Cook made a sack lunch for me, Silver and I galloped out to the forest. There was no sign of Cinderella. Well, I had to check on the progress of the lumberjacks felling trees for the new stable anyway (and race Silver a little bit, just to see how fast we could go).

Then, at dinner, Mother reminded me that the Lady Prescott and her daughter will be visiting tomorrow. She's always arranging these meetings, hoping that I will meet a girl and get married soon. "And Stephen," she added pointedly, "please behave yourself this time."

I think she was referring to the incident with Lady Marie and the loose thread. I guess I shouldn't have pulled on it, but how could I predict that Rover would get tangled when he jumped up to lick her? (I still remember the look on her face. It was worth the scolding Mother gave me.)

June 11

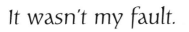

It wasn't my fault.

The Lady Prescott and her daughter Jane arrived in a carriage, but the driver didn't see the hole I had been digging to plant a Magnolia tree. Jane was carrying a mushroom-bacon casserole, and I guess someone had let Rover off his leash. I thought it was a good thing Cook made plenty of blackberry scones, because her blackberry scones are so delicious, you couldn't eat one and stay mad.

I was mistaken. Lady Prescott didn't know she was allergic to blackberries, and I didn't know Rover was allergic to mushrooms. Everyone stayed mad alright—at me.

I tried to cheer Jane up, but she kept crying.

I don't think I'll be proposing marriage to Jane anytime soon. Mother will have to invite someone else next time.

June 19

I saw Cinderella again today! I was out inspecting a section of broken fence when she came into view. She was carrying a basket of wet clothes that she hung out to dry. As I watched, she walked off and returned with two buckets of water. That's when I saw that she was standing next to a vegetable garden.

She picked lettuce, carrots, and tomatoes. She dug a pile of potatoes. She pulled weeds from the bed. Then she sat down and cleaned, peeled, and cut everything. I had to leave when Silver got hungry. By that time Cinderella was already pulling down her dry laundry.

It looked like there was enough food and laundry there for an entire family.

June 20

I asked Father today if he knew the family that lives by the edge of the woods. He said a good friend of his, Mr. Thompson, had lived there with his wife and daughter. The little girl, he remembered, was always running around chasing butterflies or the family's chickens. Then, one day, her mother fell ill and died.

Mr. Thompson eventually remarried a woman with two daughters of her own. Not long after that, he too died, leaving his new wife to take care of three daughters. Father said he hasn't seen them since, though he often wondered how the girl was doing. But when I asked, he couldn't remember her name. I wonder if she is my Cinderella.

June 21

I suppose Father told Mother about our conversation yesterday, because she has invited Mrs. Thompson and her daughters to tea tomorrow! I spent the day filling the hole in the driveway. I also promised to put Rover on his leash, and Cook has promised to make plain scones.

Mother's meddling has finally helped me meet the girl for me!

June 22

What a disappointment. When the Thompsons arrived yesterday, I peeked through the curtains as their carriage drove up and watched in horror as only two girls got out. Neither of them was Cinderella! What happened? Where was she?

I tried to be polite during tea, but the two sisters were just incredibly dull. They never stopped talking about fabrics and parties. I tried to ask if they had another sister, but Mother was shooting me those looks that make me keep my mouth shut.

June 27

Mother has decided to throw a gala ball for the entire kingdom. She says it is to be a mid-summer's party, but I know the real reason for the ball: she tired of hosting unsuccessful teas and is hoping there will be so many girls at the ball that I will meet at least one that I like. I don't want to spoil her enthusiasm, but unless the mysterious Cinderella appears, I'm not very interested in her party.

July 1

I have been avoiding Mother for days. She just won't stop talking about preparations for the gala. What do I care about flower arrangements and buffet menus? So I volunteered to take Rover along the edge of the woods looking for truffles. While Rover sniffed for those mushrooms she likes so much, I kept an eye out for Cinderella. Neither of us had much luck.

July 15

I thought the gala was going to be a bore, but it turned out to be quite interesting.

The evening started off badly. The two Thompson sisters arrived early and cornered me into two dances each. They would not stop following me around the ballroom when I tried to talk to my pals, so I waited until they went off to the powder room together and slipped out the side door. I decided to walk down to the new stable to see Silver and enjoy my freedom for a while.

On the way there, whom should I run into but my very own Cinderella! I'm not sure what she was doing in the bushes, but believe me, she was just as startled to see me as I was to see her. She was wearing a different dress from the one I saw last time, but it seemed just as old and worn. Without thinking, I asked her why she was not at the ball.

"Oh, I couldn't go," she said shyly, looking at her old dress. "I didn't really have time to get ready. I was… finishing up some housework." She told me she had walked through the woods from her home to peek at the ball and watch people dancing. So she did live in the house at the edge of the wood! I wondered if having to finish housework was the real reason she wasn't dancing at the ball in a beautiful gown like her stepsisters.

"There isn't anything that exciting going on," I told her. She looked like she didn't believe me, so I told her about the Thompson sisters who were probably at that very moment searching high and low for me. She laughed, and her smile made her just as beautiful as I imagined. We sat with Silver and talked for hours. I know now that she likes riding horses, she doesn't like to do laundry, and her real name is Cynthia. I think I will still call her Cinderella anyway.

At midnight, there was a ruckus up by the house so we ran up to see what happened. We got there just in time to see the Thompson sisters dive into a carriage and tear off into the night, the wheels of the carriage barely touching the ground as they bounced away. It's a good thing I filled that hole in the driveway.

When they were gone and the crowd had gone back inside, I saw something glittering in the driveway. I stepped closer and saw that it was a beautiful shoe made of glass. I guess it belonged to one of Cinderella's sisters, but I hadn't paid any attention to their feet earlier, so I wasn't sure. I turned to Cinderella to ask her if she knew, but she was gone. I will have to visit the Thompson house and get to the bottom of this.

July 16

The whole kingdom is in an uproar over nothing. Someone in the palace overheard me talking about finding the owner of that stupid glass shoe, and now everyone thinks that I have fallen in love with the young lady who wore it. It's no use trying to explain. Every home in the kingdom is expecting me to visit at any moment to see if the shoe fits someone in their household. What an absurd idea! I had better lay low for a few days.

July 19

I couldn't wait any longer. I rode out to the Thompson house this morning to see Cinderella again, and brought the glass shoe along to return to her stepsister.

When I first arrived, I thought the Thompsons were having a party for someone. Then I realized they were waiting for me! But it was too late. If my mouth hadn't been full, I could have explained about the shoe. If I hadn't been holding the duller of the Thompson girls in my arms, I could have run away. Lucky Rover got away in time.

"Oh, Prince Stephen, I knew you would find me," swooned the one with the shoe.

All I could reply was, "Mmmph."

The other one chimed in, "we knew you wouldn't forget us. When you marry my sister, mother and I will come to the castle to stay as well. We don't have a maid, but I'm sure you can appoint someone once we get there, right?"

"Mmmph," I said.

Once I had swallowed, I broke in as politely as I could, "Excuse me, Ma'am, but I was actually coming to see if Cynthia is available this morning?" And before I could blink, Cinderella's sister leapt out of my arms, and Mrs. Thompson snatched her cake and gifts away. The two sisters stormed off in a huff.

"Oh," said Mrs. Thompson. "You're looking for her."

Just then, we heard someone whistling a jaunty tune, and coming down the path was Cinderella herself, carrying a basket of laundry. I was so happy to see her I forgot to speak.

Cinderella spoke first. "Good morning, Prince Stephen. I hear you are searching for the owner of the glass slipper." She said this politely, and then she winked and continued, "I hope you found the girl you were looking for."

"I most certainly did find the right girl, miss," I replied.

"Right girl my foot," muttered Mrs. Thompson under her breath.

I nudged the laundry basket closer to Mrs. Thompson and asked Cinderella, "Would you care to accompany me for a ride by the creek?"

Cinderella looked at the laundry, then at her stepmother. "I would love to," she said.

As soon as we were out of sight of the cottage, Cinderella yelled, "Race you to the creek!" and galloped off. I couldn't believe how fast she could ride! I was barely able to keep up with her.

When we stopped to rest, I pulled a small packet out of my pocket. "I brought a little something for the ride," I said as I handed it to her. She peeked in and smiled.

"I love blackberry scones!"